The Princess and the Packet of FROZEN Peas

For my favourite Ps, Pippa and Polly. T.W.

For my two ugly stepsisters, Sofie and Simone. S.deG.

First published in 2009 by Scholastic Australia
This edition first published in 2009 by Scholastic Children's Books
Euston House, 24 Eversholt Street
London NW1 1DB
a division of Scholastic Ltd
www.scholastic.co.uk
London ~ New York ~ Toronto ~ Sydney ~ Auckland
Mexico City ~ New Delhi ~ Hong Kong

ISBN 978 1407 11145 2

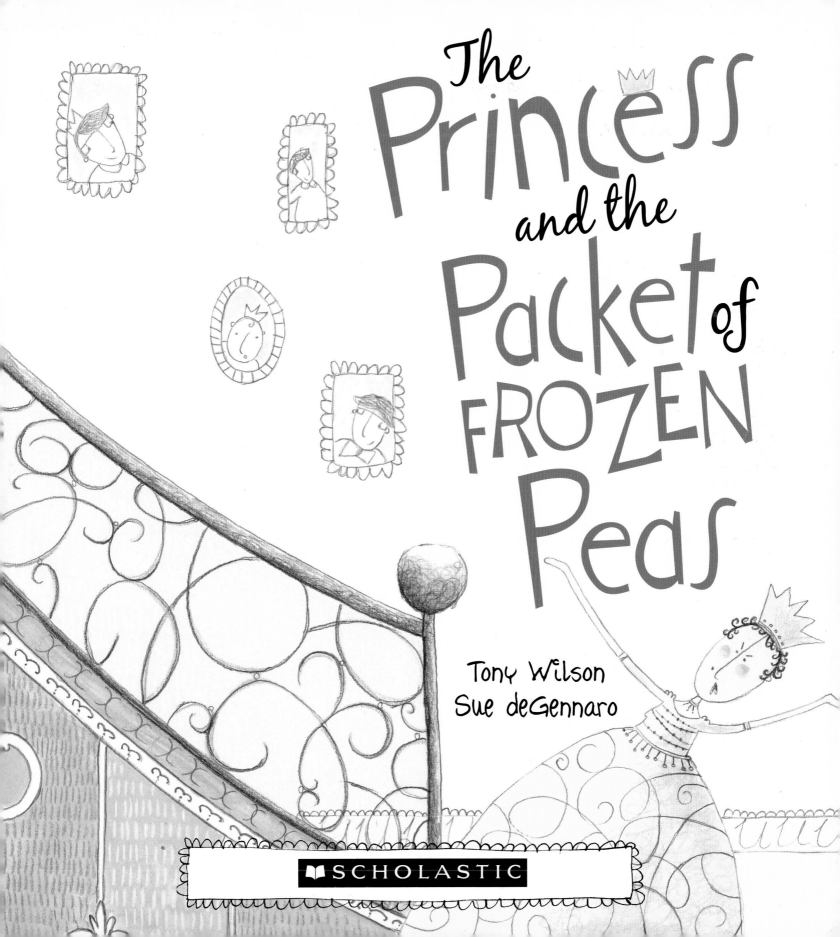

The Princess and the Packet of FROZEN Peas

Tony Wilson
Sue deGennaro

SCHOLASTIC

Once upon a time

there was a **prince** called **Henrik** who wanted very much to fall in *love* and get married.

He was an **outdoorsy** type, and hoped that the *princess* he married would like hockey and camping.

There were many girls who wanted to marry a *prince*. Every time **Henrik** left the palace, groups of screaming girls would yell, 'Oh my goodness, it's him!'

and throw flowers in his general direction.

Henrik decided to ask his brother for advice.

'The most important thing is to make sure she is a *real princess*,' Prince Hans said.

'A real princess is very *beautiful* and very *sensitive*. When I met my wife, *Princess Eva*, I made a stack of twenty mattresses and twenty eiderdowns. Then I put a single pea under the bottom mattress. If a girl complains about feeling the pea through mattresses and eiderdowns, she must be a *real princess*.'

'Did *Princess Eva* complain?' **Prince Henrik** asked.
'You bet—she complained a lot,' said *Prince Hans*.

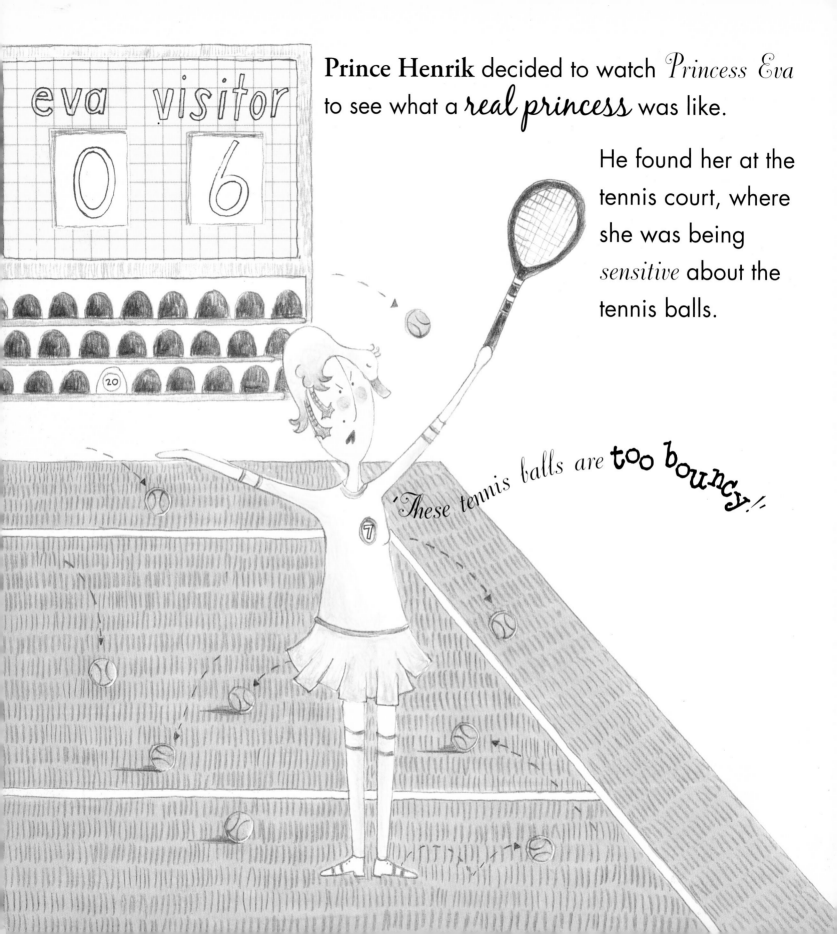

eva visitor

0 6

Prince Henrik decided to watch *Princess Eva* to see what a **real princess** was like.

He found her at the tennis court, where she was being *sensitive* about the tennis balls.

'These tennis balls are **too bouncy!**'

He followed her to the driveway and saw her being *sensitive* about her new sports car.

'This isn't the car I wanted! I wanted one with drink holders. And yellow!'

Prince Henrik wondered whether perhaps
Princess Eva was a little too *sensitive*.

Prince Henrik decided
he didn't want to marry
a *real princess* like
Princess Eva. He wanted to
marry the exact opposite.

She didn't have to be
beautiful or *sensitive*.
She just had to like hockey
and camping and have a
nice smile.

And so **Prince Henrik** came up with a plan.

Whenever a *girl* came to stay,
he offered to make up the guest room.

Instead of twenty mattresses,
Henrik found one thin camping mattress.

Instead of twenty eiderdowns,
Henrik found one old sleeping bag.

And instead of a single pea,
the **prince** decided to use a whole
packet of FROZEN PEAS.

Many young girls visited, but none passed the test.

'You won't believe this.
        I found PEAS in my bed.'

'I couldn't sleep at all!
    There was a massive
        lump under the mattress.'

'What's the deal with the
        packet of FROZEN PEAS?'

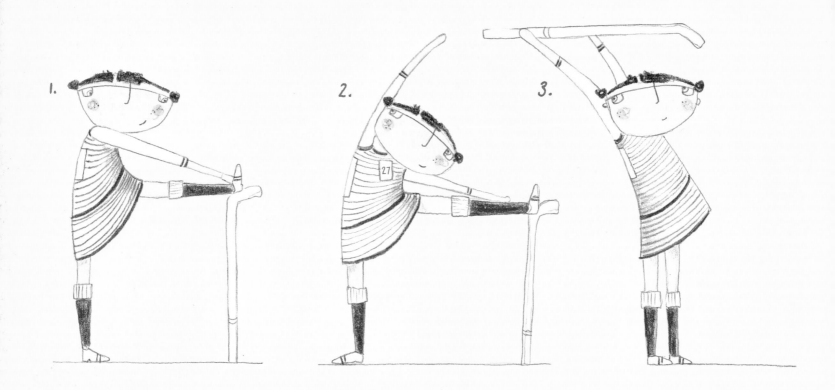

1. 2. 3.

Then one morning **Henrik**'s old schoolfriend **Pippa** came to stay.

They had a great day riding horses, playing hockey and spying on *Princess Eva* as she complained about everything in the **palace**.

'If she's a *real princess*,' Henrik joked, 'I want to marry the opposite.'

Henrik and **Pippa** laughed. For the first time **Prince Henrik** noticed what a lovely laugh she had.

That night
    he decided to test her with
        the packet of FROZEN PEAS.

The following morning **Henrik** sat in the corridor outside the guest room.

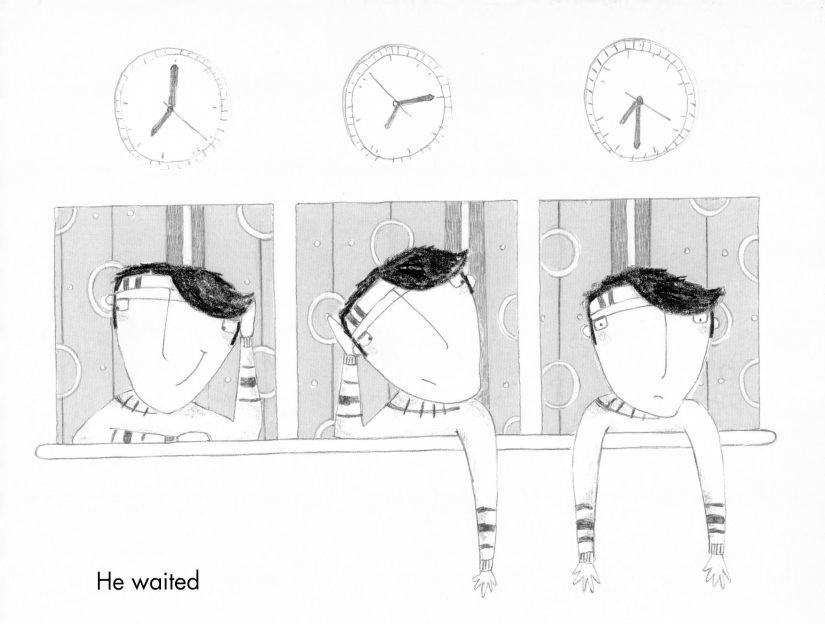

He waited

and waited

and waited.

Finally **Pippa** emerged, yawning.

'How did you sleep?'
asked **Henrik**.

'Fantastically well, thank you,' said **Pippa**,
handing him a packet of mushy peas.

'I found this under the mattress last night.

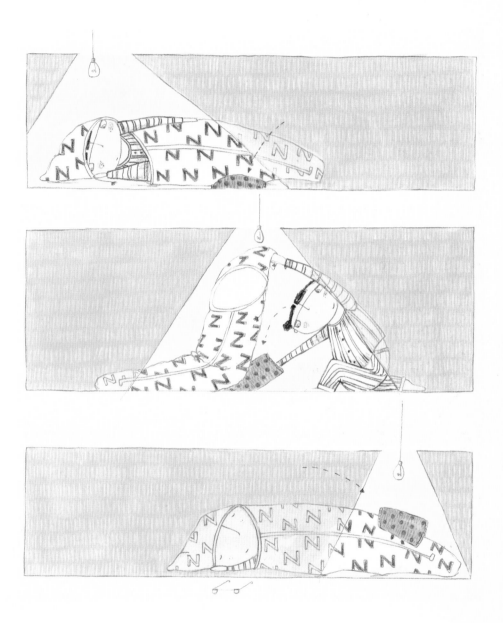

'It was the perfect icepack. I had a bit of a sore shin from playing *hockey*.'

The **prince** beamed. **Pippa** beamed back.

She had a lovely gap between her two front teeth.

'Will you marry me?' asked **Prince Henrik**.

'But I'm not a real princess,' Pippa answered.

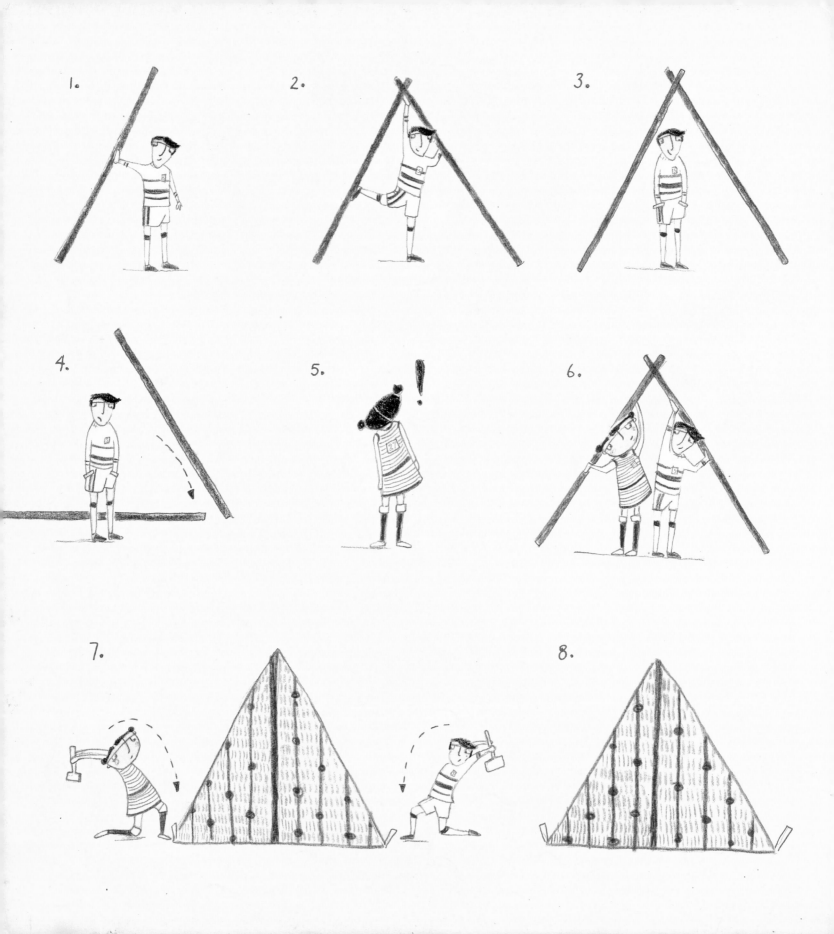

1.

2.

3.

4.

5.

6.

7.

8.